STAR TREK

THE NEXT GENERATION™

CLASSIC QUOTES

This is an officially licensed book by Appleseed Press Book Publishers LLC

13 Digit ISBN: 978-1-60433-295-7
10 Digit ISBN: 1-60433-295-6

This book may be ordered by mail from the publisher. Please include $4.95 for postage and handling.

Please support your local bookseller first!

Books published by Cider Mill Press Book Publishers are available at special discounts for bulk purchases in the United States by corporations, institutions, and other organizations. For more information, please contact the publisher.

 Cider Mill Press Book Publishers LLC
12 Port Farm Road
Kennebunkport, Maine 04046

Visit us on the web!
www.appleseedpress.com

Design by Ponderosa Pine Design, Vicky Vaughn Shea

Other photography ©2012 Shutterstock: pages 4–5 file404, losw; pages 16–17 Janos Levente; pages 18–19 Joe West; page 32 sdecoret; page 41 Albert Barr; page 43 jason2009; page 74 kanate; page 86 fixer00; page 96 sdecoret

Printed in China

2 3 4 5 6 7 8 9 0

INTRODUCTION

STAR TREK: THE NEXT GENERATION: CLASSIC QUOTES BOOK

"I have found that humans value their uniqueness, that sense that they are different from everyone else."
—Data to Worf "Second Chances"

An android with no concept of emotion comments on the nature of humanity to an alien with an oversized forehead and an aggressive disposition. It could be the makings of a joke, but conversations like this happen all the time in the *Star Trek* universe.

Science fiction works best when it turns a mirror on humanity and reflects us back at ourselves showing the good and the bad, the beauty and the blemishes. This is what has always made science fiction stories so much deeper than simple whiz-bang adventures of unusual aliens locked in exciting space battles. That concept forms the cornerstone of the *Star Trek* franchise and can be seen across all six of the television series and the multiple movies, with arguably one of the strongest examples being *Star Trek: The Next Generation*.

Gene Roddenberry's original pitch for *Star Trek* called it "a *Wagon Train* to the stars." His idea took the popular western troupe of pioneers braving an unknown frontier and moved the setting from the Earth-bound American West to space. Desilu Productions—co-owned by Lucille Ball and Desi Arnaz—bought the idea and sold it to NBC. These futuristic pioneers would search out new life and new civilizations as they boldly went where no man had gone before.

Star Trek first aired on Thursday, September 8, 1966 with the *U.S.S. Enterprise* NCC-1701 under the command of Captain James T. Kirk, as portrayed by William Shatner. The diverse cast also included Leonard Nimoy as Commander Spock playing a Vulcan/Human hybrid raised in an emotionally detached race who served as a counterpoint to his more sensitive human peers. The crew encountered guest aliens each week that allowed the writers to comment on topical issues of the sixties including war, religion, politics, and race relations through allegories from futuristic societies other than our own.

Star Trek initially enjoyed high ratings, winning its timeslot with the premier episode, but ultimately came in 52nd place (out of 94 programs) by the end of the season. NBC had considered canceling the show after the first year but it received a reprieve thanks to the effort of Lucille Ball in talks with network executives. It continued through two more seasons with the series eventually cancelled after seventy-nine episodes. But that was only the beginning of *Star Trek*'s storied history.

Paramount Studios, the company that bought Desilu, sold the syndication rights to *Star Trek* to help recoup the production losses. Reruns began in the fall of 1969 and the series quickly developed an intense cult following growing even more popular than it had been during its initial run. A fan movement and letter-writing campaign developed to get *Star Trek* back on the air in the early seventies. The interest was initially met with an animated series in 1974 before an attempt was made at a second live-action television series a few years later with *Star Trek: Phase II*. But the success of the film *Star Wars* led to the TV plans being scrapped in exchange for movies. *Star Trek: The Motion Picture* was released in 1979 ushering in a film franchise that sated the appetites of the fans for a while, but the demand for *Star*

Trek to return to television grew stronger in the eighties.

On October 10, 1986, Paramount finally gave the fans what they'd wanted since the early seventies, announcing production on a new series called *Star Trek: The Next Generation*. But the reaction to the news was mixed. There was a natural excitement for more stories set in the familiar universe, but there was also fear among the fans that the people behind the series wouldn't understand what had worked with the original. That the focus on humanity would be overlooked in exchange for exciting space battles and bizarre characters in a different universe than the one they already knew and loved. Even *Star Trek*'s creator, Gene Roddenberry, had been slow to come onboard the project prior to the announcement. Eventually "The Great Bird of the Galaxy," as Roddenberry was called, realized his stewardship was necessary to ensure that the new series followed his vision. With the originator signed on, the show went into preproduction and premiered on September 28, 1987.

Star Trek: The Next Generation, known more commonly as *TNG*, was set approximately a century after the original series. It featured a new starship and crew led by Captain Jean-Luc Picard

(Patrick Stewart) and Commander William Riker (Jonathan Frakes). Lieutenant Commander Data, as played by Brent Spiner, would fill the Spock role in the show as an android devoid of emotion commenting on the human condition as the crew of the U.S.S. *Enterprise* NCC-1701-D explored the stars. That journey, however, experienced some initial turbulence.

Star Trek and its subsequent films had established that the future was a near utopian place. War, poverty, crime, and hunger had been eradicated on Earth. Humans were members of a United Federation of Planets, a collection of alien worlds interested in exploring the universe for enlightenment, not for conquering. Sure, Kirk and his *Enterprise* crew encountered dangers in space, but the aliens they met—both good and evil—provided a counterpoint to the perfect human society of the future. Gene Roddenberry insisted that *TNG* continue that positive outlook for the future. The edict was both a blessing and a curse.

The first few seasons of *Star Trek: The Next Generation* were a challenge to the writers and there was considerable turnover among the staff. At times, that ideal utopia of the Federation became an impediment to the creation of drama required for a weekly television series. The perfect *Enterprise* crewmembers were in danger of becoming one-dimensional characters. Any flaws were relegated to the weekly guests, often placing the Starfleet officers in the role of teacher, preaching about the benefits of their perfect society.

Aliens were often relied on to provide the drama, as they had before. A hundred years after the time of Kirk, Starfleet had journeyed deeper into space forming new alliances. The Klingons had gone from bitter enemies to tentative allies, evolving into a warrior race that placed honor above all else. The Romulans, however, could still be counted on for deceit and betrayal. The series introduced the Ferengi—who began as aggressive but became opportunistic—and the Cardassians who lived under a military dictatorship. Additional new civilizations still introduced the kinds of issues that served up object lessons for the television audience. The best of these aliens were used to generate great moral dilemmas, while the less successful ones resulted in somewhat preachy oratory.

Many cite the third season—particularly the finale incorporating the Borg, a cybernetic race that had lost all traces of its humanity—as the point where *TNG* found its footing. Although there had certainly been standout episodes in the first few seasons, Captain Picard's assimilation into the Borg in "The Best of Both Worlds, Part I" was the point the series finally gelled. This incident would affect the captain for years to come as Starfleet met the first seemingly insurmountable enemy, one that was unable to comprehend anything about true humanity. The story allowed for a deeper exploration of Picard's character with the follow up episode "Family" expanding on his history and future. This new story path allowed for internal drama among the regular characters in addition to the external drama provided by the guest aliens.

Star Trek: The Next Generation ran on television for seven seasons, ending on May 23, 1994 before accepting the reins of the film franchise from its predecessor. It boasted the highest ratings of any of the *Star Trek* series before or since, becoming the number-one syndicated show on television during the last few years of its original run. *TNG* also received critical praise, earning multiple awards including a Peabody Award for Outstanding Television Programming for the episode "The Big Goodbye" and an Emmy nomination for Best Dramatic

Series during its final season.

At the show's best, it produced standout episodes that have been counted among the top television episodes of all time. Even at its weakest, it still created memorable moments that have become part of popular culture. Many of these memories are captured in the dialogue quoted within the pages of this book. Whether heartwarming and moving or lighthearted and comic, *Star Trek: The Next Generation* has become a classic in its own right boldly going where no man— where no *one*—has gone before.

Let's see what's out there.
Picard to Riker "Encounter at Farpoint"

— Paul Ruditis, Star Trek Author

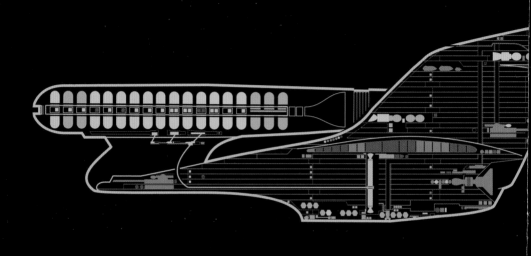

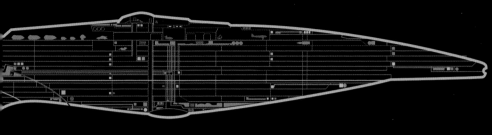

"FATE PROTECTS FOOLS,

LITTLE CHILDREN AND SHIPS

NAMED ENTERPRISE."

–William Riker, "Contagion"

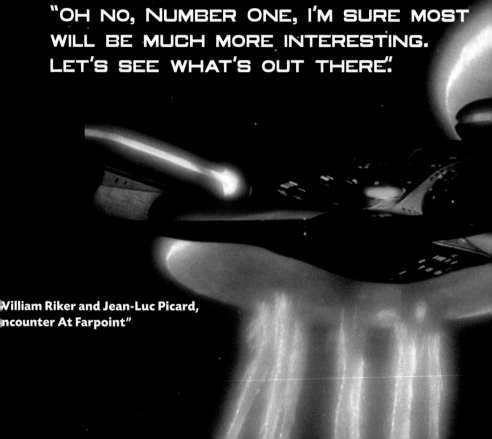

JUST HOPING THIS ISN'T THE USUAL WAY
UR MISSIONS WILL GO, SIR."

"OH NO, NUMBER ONE, I'M SURE MOST
WILL BE MUCH MORE INTERESTING.
LET'S SEE WHAT'S OUT THERE."

William Riker and Jean-Luc Picard,
ncounter At Farpoint"

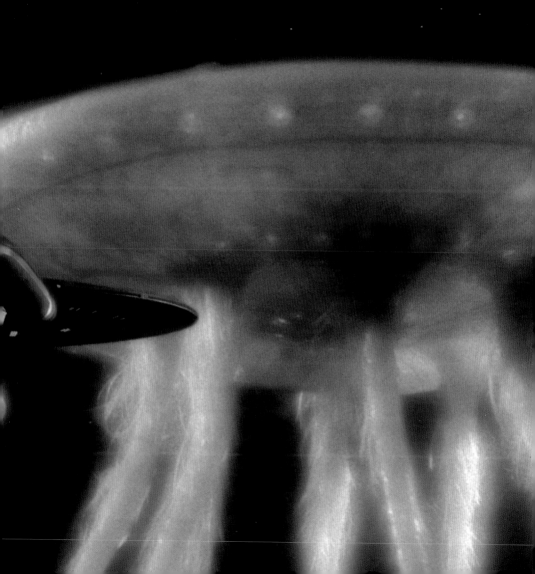

"ENG

AGE."

–Jean-Luc Picard, "Encounter At Farpoint"

"THINGS ARE ONLY IMPOSSIBLE, UNTIL THEY'RE NOT."

–Jean-Luc Picard to Data, "When the Bough Breaks"

"THE REAL SECRET IS TURNING DISADVANTAGE INTO ADVANTAGE."

—Riva, "Loud as a Whisper"

"You are fully functional, aren't you?"

"In every way, of course."

–Tasha Yar to Data, "The Naked Now"

"I am superior, sir, in many ways.
But I would gladly give it up, to be human."

"Nice to meet you, Pinocchio."

–Data and William Riker, "Encounter At Farpoint"

"*Tea. Earl Grey. Hot.*"

—Jean-Luc Picard to replicator, "Contagion"

"MAKE IT SO, NUMBER ONE."

—Jean-Luc Picard to William Riker,
"Encounter At Farpoint"

"IF BEING HUMAN IS
NOT SIMPLY A MATTER
OF BEING BORN FLESH
AND BLOOD . . . IF IT IS
INSTEAD A WAY OF
THINKING, ACTING . . .
AND FEELING . . . THEN
I AM HOPEFUL THAT
ONE DAY I WILL
DISCOVER MY OWN
HUMANITY. UNTIL THEN,
COMMANDER MADDOX,
I WILL CONTINUE . . .
LEARNING, CHANGING,
GROWING . . . AND TRYING
TO BECOME MORE
THAN WHAT I AM."

–Data to Commander Maddox, "Data's Day"

IS FUTILE."

—The Borg, "The Best of Both Worlds, Part II"

"MY FRIEND DATA YOU SEE THINGS WITH THE WONDER OF A CHILD. AND THAT MAKES YOU MORE HUMAN THAN ANY OF US."

–Tasha Yar Hologram, "Skin of Evil"

"CAPTAIN, DO YOU KNOW WHAT YEAR THIS IS?"

"OF COURSE I DO. IT'S 2278"

—Jean-Luc Picard and Morgan Bateson "Cause and Effect

"I WOULD RATHER DIE AS THE MAN I WAS . . . THAN LIVE THE LIFE I JUST SAW."

—Jean-Luc Picard to Q, "Tapestry"

"THINKING ABOUT WHAT YOU CAN'T CONTROL ONLY WASTES ENERGY AND CREATES ITS OWN ENEMY."

—Worf to Wesley Crusher, "Coming of Age"

"I was driving starships while your great grandfather was still in diapers."

—Montgomery Scott to Geordi La Forge, "Relics"

"FEDERATION SHIP
ENTERPRISE, SURRENDER
AND PREPARE TO
BE BOARDED."

"THAT WILL BE THE DAY!"

–Klingon Captain and Jean-Luc Picard,
"Yesterday's Enterprise"

"WOULD YOU LIKE TO TALK ABOUT WHAT'S BOTHERING YOU . . . OR WOULD YOU LIKE TO BREAK SOME MORE FURNITURE?"

–Deanna Troi to Worf, "Birthright"

"I protest!
I Am Not a
Merry Man!"

–Worf, "Qpid"

"Well, this is a new ship, but she's got the right name."

–Dr. McCoy to Data, "Encounter At Farpoint"

"Your ambushes would be more successful if you bathed more often."

–Worf to Brull, "The Vengeance Factor"

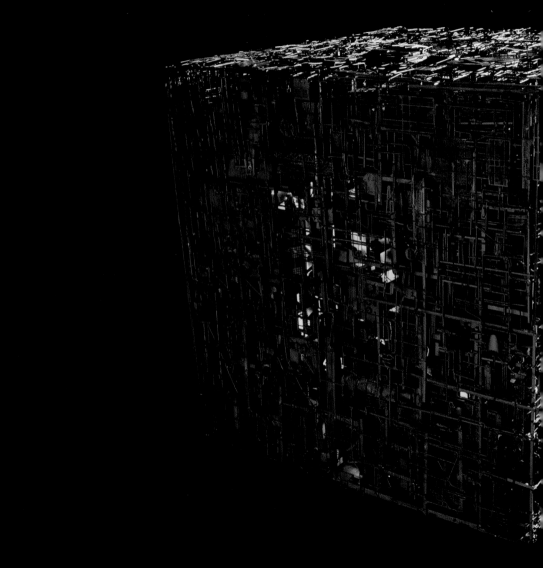

"THE BORG ARE THE ULTIMATE USER."

—Q, "Q-Who?"

"How sad, dear brother. You make me wish I were an only child"

—Data to Lore, "Datalore"

"IRONICALLY, YOU MAY KNOW SAREK BETTER THAN HIS OWN SON DOES. MY FATHER AND I NEVER CHOSE TO MELD."

"I OFFER YOU THE CHANCE TO TOUCH WHAT HE SHARED WITH ME."

—Spock to Picard, "Unification, Part II"

"COULD YOU PLEASE CONTINUE THE PETTY BICKERING? I FIND IT MOST INTRIGUING."

–Data, "Haven"

"I'VE BEEN TOLD THAT PATIENCE IS SOMETIMES A MORE POWERFUL WEAPON THAN A SWORD."

—Worf, "Redemption"

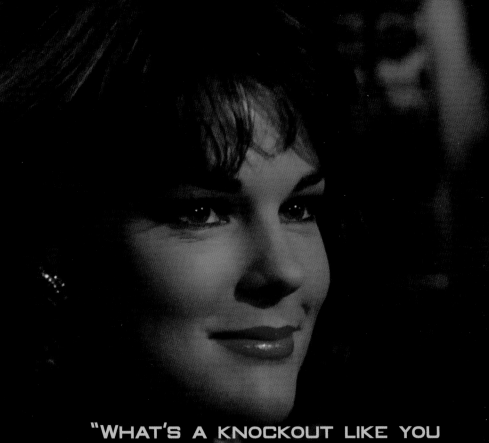

"WHAT'S A KNOCKOUT LIKE YOU
DOING IN A COMPUTER-GENERATED
GIN-JOINT LIKE THIS?"

–William Riker to Minuet, "11001001"

*"So you mean I'm drunk?
I feel strange, but also good."*

—Wesley Crusher, "The Naked Now"

"DO YOU HEAR THE CRY OF THE WARRIOR, CALLING YOU TO BATTLE, CALLING YOU TO GLORY LIKE A KLINGON?"

—Gowron, "Redemption, Part I

"*Captain. I've always known the risks that come with a Starfleet uniform. If I'm to die in one, I'd like my death to count for something.*"

—Tasha Yar, "Yesterday's Enterprise"

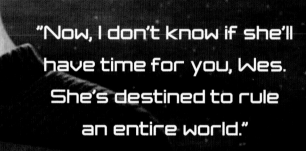

"Now, I don't know if she'll have time for you, Wes. She's destined to rule an entire world."

—William Riker to Wesley Crusher, "The Dauphin"

"IF THERE'S NOTHING WRONG WITH ME ... MAYBE THERE'S SOMETHING WRONG WITH THE UNIVERSE!"

—Dr. Beverly Crusher,
"Remember Me"

"i'M NOT GOOD IN GROUPS. iT'S DIFFICULT TO WORK IN A GROUP WHEN YOU'RE OMNIPOTENT."

–Q to Data, "Deja Q"

"COMFORTABLE CHAIR."

–William Riker and Worf, "The Emissary"

"WITH THE FIRST LINK,
THE CHAIN IS FORGED.
THE FIRST SPEECH CENSORED,
THE FIRST THOUGHT FORBIDDEN,
THE FIRST FREEDOM DENIED,
CHAINS US ALL IRREVOCABLY."

–Jean-Luc Picard, "The Drumhead"

"Darmok, and Jalad
. . . at Tanagra"

–Dathon, "Darmok"

"Cha Worf Toh'gah-nah lo Pre'tOk"

—Enterprise crew to Worf, "Parallels"

"O'BRIEN, TAKE A NAP.
YOU DIDN'T SEE ANY
OF THIS, YOU'RE NOT
INVOLVED."

"RIGHT, SIR. I'LL JUST
BE STANDING OVER
HERE, DOZING OFF."

–William Riker to Miles O'Brien, "Pen Pals"

"Eaten any good books lately?"

–Q to Worf, "Deja Q"

"So you will understand when I say, 'Death is that state in which one exists only in the memory of others . . . which is why it is not an end.' No goodbyes. Just good memories. Hailing frequencies closed, sir."

–Tasha Yar to Jean-Luc Picard,
"Skin of Evil"

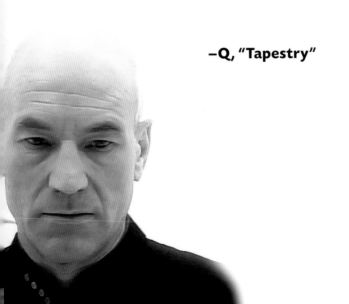

"You're dead, this is the afterlife—

and I'm God."

–Q, "Tapestry"

"HE GOT TURNED INTO A SPIDER AND NOW HE HAS A DISEASE NAMED AFTER HIM"

"I'D BETTER CLEAR MY CALENDAR FOR THE NEXT FEW WEEKS"

—**Beverly Crusher to Troi, "Genesis"**

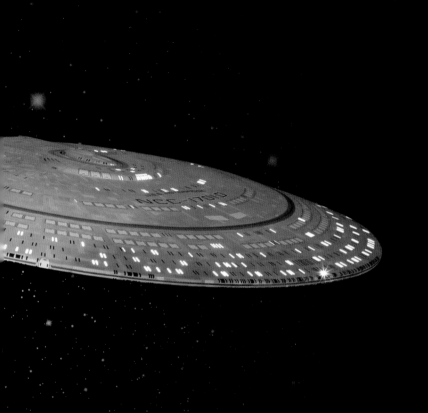

"LET'S MAKE SURE HISTORY NEVER FORGETS THE NAME ENTERPRISE."

–Jean-Luc Picard, "Yesterday's Enterprise"

"YOU'RE SO STOLID. YOU WEREN'T LIKE THAT BEFORE THE BEARD."

–Q to William Riker, "Deja Q"

"A MALFUNCTION . . .
EMOTIONAL AWARENESS".

–Jean-Luc Picard, "The Offspring"

"I mean, I ... I am the guy who writes down things to remember to say when there's a party, and then when he finally gets there, he winds up alone, in the corner, trying to look comfortable examining a potted plant."

–Reginald Barclay, "Hollow Pursuits"

"Not even a bite on the cheek for old times' sake?"

—K'Ehleyr to Worf, "Reunion"

Space ...

the final frontier.

These are the voyages of the
starship Enterprise. Its continuing
mission: to explore strange new
worlds, to seek out new life
and new civilizations, to
boldly go where no one
has gone before.

—Jean-Luc Picard

ABOUT CIDER MILL PRESS BOOK PUBLISHERS

Good ideas ripen with time. From seed to harvest, Cider Mill Press brings fine reading, information, and entertainment together between the covers of its creatively crafted books. Our Cider Mill bears fruit twice a year, publishing a new crop of titles each spring and fall.

Visit us on the Web at
www.cidermillpress.com

or write to us at
12 Port Farm Road
Kennebunkport, Maine 04046